BAKER'S DOZEN

#6

PATTY'S BIG PROBLEM

Suzanne Weyn

A
LITTLE APPLE
PAPERBACK

SCHOLASTIC INC.
New York Toronto London Auckland Sydney

ISBN 0-590-43564-7

12 11 10 9 8 7 6 5 4 3 2 1   2 3 4 5 6 7/9

Printed in the U.S.A.   28

First Scholastic printing, August 1992

For my wonderful friend, the real-life
Adrienne C. Baker,
with tons of love.

1

Problems

EIGHT-YEAR-OLD PATTY BAKER stood in the middle of the living room. "Has anybody seen Dixie?" she asked. Her brothers and sisters paid no attention to her.

For one thing, they didn't hear her. Miss Peabody, the part-time housekeeper, was vacuuming the dining room, which was next to the living room. The Bakers' vacuum was old and *very* loud.

Besides the noise, the Baker kids didn't pay attention to Patty for another reason.

They were too busy doing different things.

Seven-year-old Howie and six-year-old Kevin were racing around the room — backwards. "We're caught in a backwards space warp!" cried Howie, pushing his glasses up onto his nose as he ran.

"Yikes! Yikes! Help!" yelled Kevin, waving his arms.

"Don't step on our stuff!" scolded Collette, who was eight. She and eight-year-old Hilary were making fancy T-shirts with puff paint, sparkles, and Day-Glo markers. Pens and scraps of material lay on the floor.

Hilary was busily kissing a white shirt she'd spread out on the coffee table. She planned to cover it with lipstick kiss marks, bows, and red sparkle paint.

Over by the fireplace, five-year-old Jack was pounding on his small electric organ. Beside him, Jojo, the family's big, black Labrador retriever, lay with his paws over his ears.

Seven-year-old Terry practiced doing a split in the middle of the floor. She got all the way to the floor, but she couldn't get back up. "Somebody help me," she called, blowing one of her blonde curls from her face.

Eight-year-old Kenny and Olivia were building a tall tower out of playing cards. "Get away!" yelled Kenny as Howie and Kevin zoomed past. The tower shifted slightly, then fluttered to the ground.

"Aaaah!" groaned Olivia, flopping down on the rug.

Sixteen-year-old Chris wore head-phones and listened to an album on the stereo. Sprawled on the other end of the couch, twelve-year-old Mark played a hand-held computer game.

"Has anybody seen Dixie?" repeated Patty.

Still, no one answered her.

"I SAID," Patty shouted at the top of her lungs, "HAS ANYONE SEEN — "

Miss Peabody suddenly snapped off the vacuum.

" — DIXIE!" Patty finished, still shout-ing.

"What are you shouting for?" Kenny asked Patty.

Patty sighed. "Mom says it's time for Dixie to take her throat medicine. She asked me to get Dixie, but I can't find her."

Mr. and Mrs. Baker were on the second floor, putting together a crib that Grannie Baker had given them as a gift. Just three weeks earlier, Mrs. Baker had come home from the hospital with a seven-pound baby girl, Adrienne Claire Baker. They called her Addie. She was the thirteenth Baker kid — and the only one of them who wasn't adopted.

"I thought she was upstairs with Mom and Dad," said Chris, pushing the headphones back on her dark hair.

"Mom thought she was down here with you guys," said Patty. "Where could she be?"

Patty ran her hand through her straight, coppery red hair. Why would Dixie go off by herself? she wondered. Dixie usually liked to be in the middle of things.

"Darn!" cried Mr. Baker from upstairs. "Now I can't find the screw for this rail!"

"I have the screws and things from Dixie's old crib in this closet," Mrs. Baker called to him from the other end of the upstairs hall. "Stay calm. The baby is fine in the bassinet for now."

That gave Patty an idea. She went to the basement door. "Dixie?" she called. Nobody answered, but Patty went down anyway.

There were a Ping-Pong table and a table soccer game in the basement. Toward the back were two old stuffed chairs near the washing machine and dryer. Behind them, Mr. Baker had built a wall to make a separate room for storage.

Patty went into the storage room. "There you are," she said to Dixie. Patty had had a feeling she'd find Dixie among her old baby things. The little girl had found the mattress from her old crib and dragged it into the middle of the floor. She lay on it playing with a worn blue teddy bear and sucking her thumb.

Patty knelt on the end of the thin mattress. "What are you doing down here?" she asked.

Dixie's big blue eyes shifted from right to left. "Nothing," she replied. "I'm pretending to be a baby," she admitted after a moment.

"I thought you liked being a big girl," said Patty.

"I don't. I like being a baby," Dixie pouted. "I wish Bonkety-head would go back to the hospital."

"Who?" Patty asked.

"Bonkety-head. That's what I call the baby."

"Why do you call her that?"

Dixie huffed impatiently, as though the answer should have been obvious. "Because she *is* a bonkety-head. She has no hair, and her head is all lumpy and her face is squishy. She's ugly."

"No, she's not," said Patty. "All babies are squishy at first. That's what Mom said. She'll get cuter."

Dixie threw up her arms. "No!" she shouted. "She's too ugly!"

Patty held out her hand to Dixie. "We'd better go upstairs. Everybody is looking for you."

"Really?" said Dixie, pleased at being the center of attention.

"It's time for your throat medicine."

"Oh." Dixie's face fell. "But my sore throat doesn't hurt anymore."

"Mom still wants you to take the medicine," said Patty, shrugging. "Don't ask me why."

Still hugging the old blue teddy, Dixie followed Patty out of the basement. "I found her!" Patty called when she got to the top of the basement stairs.

"Where were you?" asked Mrs. Baker, hurrying out of the kitchen. She'd joined the search when she heard Dixie was missing. Mrs. Baker's honey-blonde hair was tied back in a ponytail. Her eyes looked tired. She hadn't slept much since the baby was born.

"She was looking at her old baby things," said Patty.

"Was Mr. Boo Bear down there?" Mrs. Baker asked, patting the stuffed blue toy. "You haven't played with him since you were very little."

"I'm still little," Dixie snapped.

At that moment, the phone rang.

"I'll get it," said Miss Peabody, hurrying into the kitchen from the dining room. She was a tall woman with sharp features. Her steely black and gray hair was pulled back in a bun.

Chris ran into the hallway. "Is it Phil?" she asked, looking hopefully into the kitchen.

Howie staggered into the hall, kissing his arm. "Oh, Phil, my love," he teased, talking to his arm. "I adore you madly."

Chris glared at him.

"No, for once it is not that messy boy, Phil," said Miss Peabody. "A Mrs. Taylor is on the phone for you, Mrs. Baker." Mrs. Taylor was the social worker who had first brought Patty to live with the

8

Bakers. Before that, Patty had stayed in foster homes and a children's shelter.

Mrs. Baker turned to Patty and smiled. "I bet this is it," she said.

"You mean my adoption will finally be final?" Patty asked excitedly. Patty had lived with the Bakers since last August. It was now May.

"It must be," her mother replied. "What else could she want?"

Patty followed Mrs. Baker into the kitchen, skipping happily. Soon she would be a real, legal Baker — forever and ever.

"Hello, Mrs. Taylor," said Mrs. Baker into the telephone.

Patty watched her mother's smile slowly fade. "What kind of problem?" she asked. "I see . . . uh-huh." The pink disappeared from Mrs. Baker's cheeks.

Problem? Patty began to feel sick. She held her breath.

Mrs. Baker hung up the phone.

"What's the matter?" Patty asked slowly.

"Sit down, sweetheart," said Mrs. Baker, looking shaken. "We have to talk."

2

Stu D. Baker

"I LOVE THE WOODS," Dixie told Patty.

"Me, too," Patty agreed.

They were walking in the woods that came right up to the driveway of their large, gray house. Patty liked to go there when she wanted to think. And right now she needed to think. Hard.

She'd wanted to be alone. But Dixie had spotted her heading into the woods and begged to come. Patty didn't have the heart to say no.

"You look sad," Dixie observed.

"It's my adoption," Patty told her. "Mrs. Taylor is going to come talk to Mom and Dad about it." Patty's voice trembled as she spoke. "There's some problem or something. She's coming tomorrow."

"Tomorrow," Dixie echoed solemnly. It was Sunday afternoon. Patty had tossed and turned all Saturday night. All she could think about was Monday, when Mrs. Taylor would arrive. What could the problem be?

They walked for a while without talking. Dixie ran ahead, looking at bugs, and yellow-green buds that were beginning to dot the trees. She'd wait for Patty to catch up and then run ahead again.

It was a beautiful day, with a blue sky and big fat clouds rolling lazily above them.

But, to Patty, the weather seemed all wrong. The sky should have been filled with threatening, rumbling thunderclouds.

Why did this have to happen? It wasn't fair! Things were going so well, too.

Just recently she'd begun calling Mr. and Mrs. Baker Mom and Dad. In the beginning, she simply tried not calling them anything. She'd make a little "ahem" noise or stand directly in front of them if she needed their attention. It just didn't feel right calling two people she barely knew Mom and Dad.

But, lately, it had started feeling right.

Even Hilary, with whom she shared a room, no longer bothered her. Well, not as much as before — Hilary could still be pretty irritating. But even when she *did* bother Patty, it was a sisterly kind of bothering. In a way, Patty had come to like it. Though she would never, ever, tell that to Hilary.

Patty remembered a time way back, when her mother was still alive. Patty had been four, almost five. It was late in the afternoon on a summer day, and Patty and her mother had built a beautiful sandcastle near the water. Patty had lined up her favorite little toy ponies at the castle doorway. It was a magical, wonderful sight.

Then a big wave crashed up on the shore. It came up further than any of the waves before it. Smash! Patty and her mother ran around madly, scooping up the floating ponies. When they turned back to their castle, it was just a lump of wet sand.

Now it was happening all over again. Mrs. Taylor was like the wave. Just when everything seemed perfect, she was coming to wash it all away.

"Hey, look!" Dixie cried. She'd broken into a run, waving her arms for balance as she slipped and slid down a steep, wooded slope.

Patty followed. At the bottom of the slope sat a very old, very rusty car. Patty had only seen cars like it in movies. It was much bigger than a modern car, with big, round fenders. The tires were all flat.

"How did it get here?" Dixie asked.

That was a good question. Trees surrounded it. The spaces in between the trees were too narrow for the car to have been driven through.

"I don't know," Patty admitted. She tried to open the doors, but they wouldn't budge. The girls looked into the windows. Patty had to hold Dixie up because she was too short to reach them.

The seats were torn and rotted. Dixie giggled, and said, "There's a plant growing in the back seat." Patty saw that the back lefthand window was a little less than halfway open. Dirt had blown in, filling a long rip in the seat. A weed had sprouted in the rip.

"Nature is weird," said Patty. "Plants seem to find a place to grow no matter what. When I was at the children's shelter, there was a dandelion growing outside my window and it was stuck in the dirt between two bricks."

She put Dixie down, and the little girl ran to the back of the car. In a minute she had scrambled into the large open trunk.

Dixie stretched out. "This is my bedroom. My own bedroom, and Bonketyhead can't sleep with me." Right now, the baby slept in Mr. and Mrs. Baker's bedroom. But Dixie had been told that she and the baby would share a room when Adrienne was bigger. Dixie did not like this idea at all.

"Come on," said Patty, holding out her hand. "We'd better get back." They'd walked far. Patty wasn't even sure if they were still on their own property.

When they got home, good smells wafted out into the backyard from the open screen door. On Sundays, the Bakers had their large meal in the middle of the day. It was always something special.

"There you are," Grannie Baker greeted them as they stepped into the kitchen. "We were just about to go out into the woods looking for you."

Patty liked Grannie Baker. She had short, peachy-colored hair and sparkly blue eyes. Grannie was always traveling and bringing back interesting things. Today she was taking a large duck from the oven. "Peking duck," she announced. Grannie had visited China and learned to cook many Chinese dishes.

"Grannie! Grannie! We found a car," Dixie said, dancing merrily around Grannie. "It's a magic car. It appeared in the middle of all these trees."

"I'd forgotten all about that old Studebaker," said Mr. Baker, coming into the kitchen. He was a tall man with wispy blond hair.

"A stupidbaker?" asked Dixie.

"Not stupidbaker, Studebaker. It's the name of the car. They don't make them anymore," Mr. Baker explained. "I've been meaning to get rid of that car for years. It was here when we bought the house."

"Hey!" said Patty, who had settled in at the long kitchen table. "The car belongs here. It's named Baker, isn't it? Stu D. Baker."

Mr. Baker smiled. Grannie laughed and ruffled Patty's hair. "She's right, Tom. It looks like you have one more Baker to deal with."

"No! Tell me I didn't hear that!" cried Hilary from the kitchen doorway. "No more kids! I'm begging!"

"Don't worry, Hilary," laughed Mr. Baker. "We have our baker's dozen. That's enough." Since the baby was born, Mr. Baker liked to say they were now a true baker's dozen. He was referring to the fact that at one time, bakers gave anyone who bought a dozen rolls a thirteenth roll for free. Thirteen of anything came to be known as a baker's dozen.

"This Baker is a car," Patty told Hilary. "We found it in the woods."

"What a relief!" sighed Hilary. She had been the first child the Bakers adopted, and she made no secret of her opinion that one child — especially a child as remarkable as herself — should have been enough.

"Dad, how did the car get there?" Patty asked.

"Believe it or not, that forest was once

a field. I found some old photos of the property in the attic. That car was abandoned in the back of the field, and through the years the trees grew all around it."

"Cool," said Patty.

Patty, Hilary, and Mr. Baker helped Grannie put the dinner things on the table. Pitchers of milk and juice, three large baskets of rolls, two salad bowls full of lettuce and tomatoes, two sets of salt and pepper shakers, and three plates of butter were set out.

Grannie went to the doorway and cupped her hand to her mouth. *"Yodel-odle-odle-aaaa-heeeee-hooooooo!"* Ever since Grannie returned from Switzerland, she liked to yodel as a signal for everyone to come to eat.

Thundering footsteps pounded down the stairs as the kids came running. Howie and Kevin raced in from the back door. Mark and Kenny collided as they both tried to get through the kitchen door at once.

"*Arf!*" barked Jojo as Mr. Baker scooped a can of dog food into his bowl.

Mrs. Baker came in with Addie in her arms. "*Wah-wah-wah!*" the baby cried suddenly.

"*Ah-ah-ahooooooooooo!*" Jojo howled.

They all covered their ears. Jojo had howled along with Addie ever since she came home from the hospital. At first they thought the crying bothered him. Then they realized Jojo was just singing along.

"She needs a diaper change," sighed Mrs. Baker. Jojo continued to howl as Mrs. Baker carried Addie from the room.

A devilish look came into Kenny's eyes. He threw his head back and imitated Jojo. "Yip-yip-ahooooooo!"

"Ahoo-ahooo-ahooo!" howled Kevin.

"Ow-ow-ow-owoooooooooooo!" Collette joined in.

Soon all the kids were howling. "Ahhh-hooooo! Ah-hooooo!"

"Okay, that's enough! Enough!" laughed Mr. Baker. The kids stopped howling and dissolved into fits of laughter.

All except Patty.

Patty was surprised to find herself biting her lip. Unexpectedly, hot tears threatened to splash down her cheeks. How could Mrs. Taylor even think of taking her away? This was her family now. Hers! She wouldn't let Mrs. Taylor spoil that. No way!

3

Mrs. Taylor's Bad News

PATTY SAT ON THE STEPS hugging her knees while Mrs. Baker held a last-minute family meeting. Twelve kids were assembled in the front hall. Baby Addie was asleep upstairs.

"Okay, now, everybody," said Mrs. Baker as she tugged at Jack's hair with a comb. "Mrs. Taylor will be here any minute. Let's show her what a polite and organized family we are."

"My neck itches," Kenny complained,

pulling the collar of his white, button-down shirt.

Mrs. Baker sighed. "I'm sorry, Kenny, but the only clean T-shirt I could find for you has the Tasmanian devil on it. I don't think that would make a good impression."

"Who cares what Mrs. Taylor thinks of us?" grumbled Mark, who sat on the bottom step sulking about having to wear his dress loafers instead of his red high-top sneakers.

"You guys!" said Olivia as she fussed with the pleats of her blue jumper. "It's just for a few hours, until Mrs. Taylor leaves."

"I agree with Mark," said Grannie, coming in from the living room. "This is a perfectly nice family. There's no need to put on airs."

"Grannie, please," said Mrs. Baker. "It can't hurt to put our best foot forward."

"Well, I'll be in the kitchen working on my recipe for pineapple upside-down cake," Grannie said.

"Has anyone seen my new tutu?" called Hilary from the top of the stairs. Hilary planned to be a ballerina someday.

Kevin and Howie punched each other and laughed.

"I know you guys hid it!" Hilary shouted.

"What do you need your tutu for now?" asked Terry.

"I want Mrs. Taylor to see that someone in this house has some culture. I thought I'd show her my latest steps."

"Hilary, I don't think that would be a good idea," Mrs. Baker objected.

"Sure it would be," said Hilary. "But these two little nerds hid my tutu. Make them — "

At that moment, the doorbell rang. Mr. Baker hurried down the stairs straightening his tie. He'd come home early from Wild Falls College where he taught, just to see Mrs. Taylor.

Mrs. Baker pulled a blue blazer from the hall closet and helped Mr. Baker into it.

The doorbell rang again.

"Coming," called Mrs. Baker, straightening the bow tying back her hair. She opened the door to Mrs. Taylor, a tall, thin woman with short reddish hair. Mrs. Taylor wore a beige suit, matching high heels, and carried an overstuffed briefcase.

"Hel-lo, Mrs. Tay-looor," the kids sang out in unison.

Slightly surprised by this greeting, Mrs. Taylor gave them a quick smile. "May I talk to you privately?" she asked Mr. and Mrs. Baker.

"Of course," said Mr. Baker. "Come into the living room."

The kids followed the adults. They perched on the furniture and stared at Mrs. Taylor, politely waiting for her to speak. Mrs. Taylor looked very uncomfortable.

"Kids, I think Mrs. Taylor wants to talk to your father and me alone," Mrs. Baker told them.

"We want to hear!" cried Dixie.

"Let's go," Chris said, taking Dixie by the hand. The rest of the kids followed. They didn't go far, though. They turned the corner of the living room and bunched up together right outside the door. They just *had* to hear what Mrs. Taylor was about to say.

Patty sat closest to the door. She bit her thumbnail anxiously as she listened.

"As you know," said Mrs. Taylor, "Patty's mother is dead, but her father is not. He abandoned Patty and her mother when Patty was just an infant. We are obliged by law to conduct a search for him before letting you legally adopt Patty."

Mrs. Baker gasped. "You found him?"

"No," said Mrs. Taylor. "We still have no idea where he is."

"Is that the problem?" Mr. Baker asked.

"Not really. Once we conduct a complete search, we can end his parental rights on the grounds of abandonment," Mrs. Taylor told them.

"Ow!" Patty had bitten her thumb so hard, it began to bleed.

"Shhhh," whispered Collette softly.

"The problem is that in conducting our search, we discovered an elderly couple living in Omaha, Nebraska. The wife is Patty's father's second cousin. It is our agency's policy to keep blood relatives together as much as possible. And since Patty's adoption isn't yet final — "

"You want to give Patty to them?" cried Mrs. Baker. "Well, you can't. I won't let — "

"Ann, please," Mr. Baker interrupted gently. "Let Mrs. Taylor finish. Is this definite, Mrs. Taylor?"

"The couple is old, and they don't really want to start raising an eight-year-old child," said Mrs. Taylor. "Yet they want to be sure she's being well cared for. They're flying in from Nebraska this week. They want to meet you and see what kind of family you are. If they're satisfied that everything is fine, then Patty can stay."

Just then, from upstairs, the baby began wailing.

"That's great," said Mrs. Baker, getting

up. "I'm sure they'll like what they see."

"*Aw-wooooooooooooooooo!*" Jojo, who had been lying under the table, began singing along with the baby.

Mrs. Taylor jumped to her feet. "Good heavens, what is that?"

"Oh, it's just the dog," Mr. Baker replied.

"Somebody shut Jojo up," Hilary whispered fiercely.

Kevin and Howie threw themselves on the howling dog, trying to grip his mouth shut. Jojo pulled away and backed up into a standing lamp.

Smash! The glass globe on the lamp crashed to the ground.

Jojo continued howling.

"Clean that up," whispered Mrs. Baker as she hurried past them on her way to get Addie.

Just then, a deafening roar drowned out the baby *and* Jojo. It was the sound of a very loud motorcycle. It sounded as if it were about to drive right through the front door.

"Phil!" Chris cried happily. She ran for the door.

Mr. Baker came in from the living room and blocked her path. "Hold it right there, young lady," he said. "I told you, you are not allowed on that motorcycle. Those things are too dangerous."

"Phil won't go out with me if I can't ride with him!" Chris objected, pushing past her father.

"Come back here," Mr. Baker cried, following her out the door.

Mrs. Taylor stepped into the hallway. "Hi, Patty," she said. "How are things going?"

Patty stopped chewing her thumb. She opened her mouth to answer Mrs. Taylor. "Hic-up!" was all she could say. Her hand flew to her mouth. "I'm f-f-f-hic-up. Fine," she managed.

"She is fine. Really fine," Hilary jumped in.

"Hic-hic-hic-up," said Patty.

For a moment, all was quiet. The baby

had stopped, Jojo had stopped, and Phil had shut his engine.

"Ahhhhh," sighed Mrs. Taylor.

"Hic," said Patty.

Mrs. Baker came down the stairs with Addie bundled in a pink blanket.

"You didn't plan on having this thirteenth baby, did you?" Mrs. Taylor noted.

"No, we didn't think we could have children," Mrs. Baker answered. "It was quite a surprise. A happy surprise."

"And you don't find thirteen to be too many?" Mrs. Taylor questioned. "After all, it's more than you planned on."

"Oh, no, we're doing just fine," Mrs. Baker assured her.

Just then, Chris threw the door open and ran tearfully up the stairs. The thunderous roar of the motorcycle filled the hall as Phil drove off. The noise startled Addie, who began to cry. The crying set off Jojo, who howled loudly.

"Just fine," Mrs. Baker repeated, speaking very loudly.

"Mmmmmmm," said Mrs. Taylor. Patty didn't like the look on her face. She wanted to tell Mrs. Taylor that everything *was* fine. She opened her mouth to speak.

"Yes, Patty?" said Mrs. Taylor.

"Hic-up!" said Patty.

Suddenly horrible black smoke billowed in from the kitchen. "Oh! Oh!" cried Grannie Baker.

Everyone ran into the kitchen in time to see Grannie pull a flaming tutu out of the oven. "I was heating up the oven," she cried as she tossed the charred pink tulle tutu into the sink. "Who put this tutu in here?"

Mrs. Taylor took a pad from her briefcase and quickly wrote something.

"Hic!" said Patty.

4

Hilary Lessons

THAT NIGHT, PATTY LAY IN BED, her eyes wide. She couldn't stop worrying. What if her relatives had been here this afternoon? Would they think she lived in a normal home? Probably not.

Across the room a soft glow shone through Hilary's blanket. She was under the covers with a flashlight, reading her latest teen fashion magazine.

"Hilary," Patty whispered.

There was no reply.

"Hilary."

Hilary flipped the covers away from her face. "What?" she snapped, annoyed.

"Forget it," said Patty.

"What, what, what!" Hilary pressed. "Now that you've made me lose my place, you might as well tell me."

"Do you think my relatives will let me stay?" Patty asked.

Hilary got out of bed and went over to Patty's bed. She flashed her light in Patty's face.

"Cut that out!" Patty whispered sharply.

"I was just looking at you," said Hilary. "I wanted to see if you look like you're being properly brought up."

"Do I?" asked Patty.

"I'm not sure," said Hilary. "You're too skinny, and your hair is a mess."

Patty tucked a strand of hair behind her ear. "It is not!"

"You don't have any special talents," Hilary went on. "Too bad you're not more like me."

Patty had to admit Hilary had a point. Hilary always made a very good impression on adults. Her hair was always set and perfectly combed. She was always well dressed. She had special manners she used just for adults, and she could always think of something to say.

For the first time, Patty wished she *were* more like Hilary. If she were, then her relatives would be sure she was doing just finc at the Bakers'.

"Could you teach me to be more like you?" Patty asked.

"Hmmm," Hilary considered. "There really is only one me."

"I know, but just some pointers," said Patty.

"All right," Hilary agreed. "For one thing, you should hold your head higher. And always keep your shoulders back."

Hilary showed Patty her chin-up-shoulders-back pose. "It's very graceful," she said, her slightly pointy nose tilted to the ceiling. "Ballerinas pose like this."

Patty did the same. Hilary was right. The pose *did* make her feel important. But her neck quickly began to feel tired. "What if I have to look down to see something?" she questioned Hilary.

"If something is on the floor, just kick it aside," Hilary advised. "Next we have to fix your voice. Yours is kind of raspy."

"It is?" Patty asked. No one had ever told her that before.

"Absolutely," Hilary confirmed. "Sometimes you sound like a boy. You should try to talk more like a girl."

"But I am a girl, and this is how I talk," Patty protested.

Hilary frowned. "Do you want me to help you or not?"

"Of course I do," said Patty. She began to speak in a soft, whispery voice. "How is this?"

"Better," said Hilary.

For the next hour, Hilary gave Patty advice on how to improve herself. Finally, Hilary yawned. "I'm tired. Wake me up a little early tomorrow, and we'll work on your appearance."

"Okay," Patty agreed. "Thanks, Hilary."

"You're welcome," said Hilary as she pulled her blanket over her shoulder and turned toward the wall.

The next morning, Hilary awoke before Patty. She stood next to her bed and shook Patty's shoulder. "Come on, get up. We have to set your hair."

Patty rubbed her eyes. "What time is it?"

"Six-thirty. You have to use the electric rollers, then I have to use them. It takes time," Hilary explained.

Sleepily, Patty sat as Hilary rolled up her hair. "Your hair is impossible," Hilary complained. "It's so thin, the rollers don't even stay in."

"Sorry," said Patty.

When Hilary took out the rollers, some of the hair was curly. Other strands were just slightly bent. "This is hopeless." Hilary sighed. Then her eyes brightened. "I know!" She took a hot-pink elastic from her top drawer. "This will work," she said. Hilary brushed all of Patty's hair to one side and tied the elastic around it. "That looks stylish, at least."

Patty wasn't so sure. "Don't you think it looks a little weird just sticking out of the side of my head like that?"

"Not at all," said Hilary. "And remember your new voice."

Hilary let Patty borrow her pink tights and matching stretch turtleneck top. She lent her a short denim skirt. "You'll have to wear your own shoes since your feet are so much larger than mine," she said. "But you do look better already."

"Really?" questioned Patty, who had never worn a dress or skirt to school before. She much preferred pants.

"Yes. And I forgot to tell you something last night. When you're dealing with adults, it's important to laugh a lot. They love it if *they* think *you* think they're funny."

"But what if they're not?" asked Patty.

"Laugh anyway. But don't laugh your old laugh. You laugh like this: 'Heeeeheeeee-he-snort-snort-heeeee.' "

"I don't snort," said Patty.

"A lot of times you do," Hilary insisted. "Instead, put your hand over your mouth and giggle like this: 'He-he-he-he-he!' "

Patty scowled. "You don't laugh like that."

"I have my own unique laugh that I'm not sharing with anyone," Hilary explained calmly.

Hilary and Patty went down to breakfast. They were the last ones there. All the other kids sat at the kitchen table eating cold cereal. "What happened to you?" Kenny asked Patty.

"I want to make a good impression on my relatives," Patty explained.

"Well, you look dumb," Kenny insisted, lifting his bowl to drink the last of the milk.

"Leave her alone," said Chris grouchily. She was still in a bad mood about Phil.

"Save us!" yelled Howie. "The Hilary

monster has begun to reproduce. Stop her before she takes over the entire planet."

"Pow-pow-pow." Kevin pretended to fire on them.

"Do I look dumb?" Patty asked Olivia.

"No. You just look like Hilary," Olivia replied.

"She doesn't look exactly like me," Hilary jumped in. "I'm just trying to help her."

"Oh, man! How weird can you get," Collette said. "But, adults *do* go crazy for Hilary. I suppose you could act like Hilary until your relatives come. Then, after they leave, you can go back to being a normal human being."

"Very funny," Hilary sniffed. "I don't see the rest of you helping Patty. All you did yesterday was make a mess of things."

"Don't worry," said Mark, grabbing his books from the table. "Everything will be fine tomorrow when your relatives come. I'll keep Jojo out in the yard with me."

"And you won't have to worry about Phil," Chris said huffily. "Dad has forbidden him to bring his motorcycle onto our property. Which is so unfair!"

"Nothing will go wrong," Olivia assured her.

"Thanks," said Patty. Her brothers and sisters were being very nice. She just hoped they were right.

5

The Worst
Birthday Party Ever

THAT AFTERNOON, PATTY CAME HOME from school in a good mood. Ms. Sherman, her teacher, had admired her outfit. Patty had smiled and said, "Thanks," in her new, whispery voice. Ms. Sherman had looked at her a little strangely then, but she hadn't criticized the new voice. Patty took that to mean she liked the new voice — it had simply surprised her.

"Hi, everyone," Mrs. Baker greeted her kids when they came in. "I need helpers.

I'm expecting seven three- and four-year-olds in the next half hour."

"Oh, that's right, Dixie's birthday party is today," said Collette. "I'll help. Man, I can't believe she's going to be four."

"I'll help, too," said Patty.

"Me three," said Olivia.

"Good enough," said Mrs. Baker. "Go help Grannie in the kitchen."

At that moment, Dixie appeared on the stairs looking very unhappy. She had on a new blue dress with a lace collar. "Mommy, I hate this dress," she said.

"But it's your party dress," replied Mrs. Baker.

Dixie pouted. "It's not mine. It used to be Terry's. I want a brand-new dress."

"Terry only wore it once," said Mrs. Baker. "It's almost new."

"It's old and ugly," Dixie said, folding her arms.

Mrs. Baker took a deep breath. "Terry, please help her find something else to wear," she said. Terry ran up the stairs.

Olivia, Collette, and Patty followed Mrs.

Baker into the kitchen. Addie had been crying all day, and now everything was behind schedule. Mrs. Baker had taken her to the doctor in the morning. The doctor told her the baby was fine. "Newborns sometimes have cranky days," she said. "Maybe she's coming down with a little cold." Right now, Addie was sleeping in the kitchen in her stroller.

Grannie Baker was icing Dixie's cake. Mrs. Baker handed Collette and Patty a bag of balloons to blow up. Olivia and Hilary set the table with paper plates and plastic forks and spoons.

"Mom!" Terry said, coming into the kitchen. "Dixie insists on wearing her new nightgown to the party. She says it's the only nice thing she has. She says Addie is the one with all the nice new clothes."

"It's her party. Let Dixie wear her nightgown, if that's what she wants," Grannie suggested.

Mrs. Baker sighed loudly. "Let me talk to her," she said, leaving the kitchen.

Soon the doorbell began ringing. Seven

little girls and boys were dropped off by their parents. Dixie still hadn't come downstairs. Neither had Mrs. Baker.

In the living room, Patty got the kids started on a game of musical chairs. In a few minutes Dixie appeared on the stairs wearing a pink flowered dress. Her pout turned into a smile as she ran to join the game. Before long, only Dixie and a four-year-old named Jessica were circling one chair.

Patty stopped the music. Jessica hopped into the chair. "Jessica is the winner," Patty announced, digging into a plastic bag for a prize.

"Wait a minute!" Dixie shouted.

Everyone turned and stared at her.

"It's my birthday. I'm the one who is supposed to win!" Dixie yelled.

"Sorry, honey," said Mrs. Baker, who had just come in from the kitchen. "It doesn't work that way."

"I'm the birthday girl!" Dixie insisted.

"You'll have the chance to win some-thing else," Mrs. Baker said, handing a small wrapped package to Jessica.

But Dixie didn't win any of the games. Not pin-the-tail-on-the-donkey, not freeze tag, and not blind man's bluff. Each time, she shouted and insisted that the birthday girl was supposed to win all the prizes.

"You don't need a prize," Patty told her. "You're getting lots of presents."

When it was time for cake, Dixie brightened. Grannie had made a beautiful cake. On top was a big blue teddy bear surrounded by chocolate icing. Everyone sang "Happy Birthday," and Dixie blew out the four candles. She seemed much happier until she bit into the cake.

"Bleecchhhh!" Dixie stuck out her tongue, still full of the blue bear icing. "What is this stuff?"

"Coconut," said Grannie. "Don't you like it? I put blue food coloring onto the white coconut."

Dixie pointed to her tongue. "Get it off," she said. "It's disgusting."

"Dixie, please," said Mrs. Baker, wiping Dixie's tongue with a wet paper towel. All the other kids began picking around the blue bear, turning their cake into piles of crumbs.

As the kids crumbled their cake, Addie began crying. "Oh, no!" Dixie moaned. "Not Bonkety-head again!"

Mrs. Baker gently rocked the stroller. Addie stopped crying. "Open some of your presents," Mrs. Baker suggested. "Patty and Olivia can hand them to you."

Eagerly, Dixie ripped open the first gift. Her bright smile quickly disappeared. "A Doodler," she grumbled, tossing the gift aside.

"Dixie," Grannie scolded. "That's a lovely present. You can draw all sorts of things with it, and it erases so you can draw something different. That's a cool gift."

"I have one already," Dixie said.

"You can always use another," Grannie said. "Thank Monique."

Dixie mumbled her thanks and took the next package from Olivia. It was a pair of pajamas with feet from Jessica. "Feet pajamas!" Dixie cried as if the gift were an insult. "Those are for babies. I'm four."

"I like feet pajamas," said Collette. "I wish they made them in my size."

Dixie looked at Collette as though she were insane. "I hate them," she insisted.

"Dixie!" Mrs. Baker scolded. "Be polite."

"Thank you, Jessica," Dixie sighed, stuffing the disappointing gift back in the box.

"*Wa-wa-waaaa*," Addie began a low whimper.

"Is she going to start screaming again?" asked Dixie.

Mrs. Baker picked up Addie. "Just open your next present," she said.

"This is a neat toy," said her friend Matthew when he saw Patty handing Dixie his package. "You don't have to worry about this one."

At first Dixie smiled when she saw the large blue water pistol. But her smile turned to a frown as she took it from the package. There was a long crack in the gun.

"Oh, boy," said Matthew. "That must have happened when I dropped it. Sorry."

"We can exchange it," said Patty.

Mrs. Baker finally got Addie to quiet down. Gently she placed her back in the stroller. But the moment Addie's head hit the cushion, her eyes popped open. *"Wah-wah-wah!"*

"Oh, be quiet!" yelled Dixie. She scooped some of the blue coconut icing off the plate at her side. *Fwap!* she lobbed it at Addie. *Plop!* It hit the baby right on the forehead.

"Waaaaaaaaaaaaaaaaaaaaaaaaaa!"

Patty quickly wiped the icing off the baby's face. In a second Mrs. Baker was firmly guiding Dixie out of her chair. "All right, Dixie," she said in a low, stern voice. "I've had about enough. Let's go to your room until you can be more pleasant."

Dixie turned beet red and burst into tears as Mrs. Baker led her from the room. "Poor Dixie," sighed Grannie, lifting Addie from the stroller.

"Goody bags!" shouted Collette, quickly

giving bags of candy and cookies to each of the kids.

Luckily it was time for the party to end. The doorbell began ringing as parents came to pick up their kids.

Mrs. Baker came downstairs and took Addie from Grannie. "Dixie has to learn that she can't behave that way," she said to Grannie.

"I know," said Grannie sadly as she cleared the table. "My little Dixie-doodle is having a hard time these days. She's not the baby anymore. It's put her in a very bad mood."

"I understand, but I can't allow her to be rude to her friends and throw cake at the baby," Mrs. Baker insisted.

"You're right," Grannie agreed.

Patty quietly slipped out of the kitchen and went to Dixie's room. "How are you feeling?" she asked.

"Terrible," replied Dixie, sitting on her bed, her face tear-stained. "This was the worst birthday ever. Mommy doesn't love

me anymore. She only loves Bonkety-
head."

"Mom made you that nice party," said
Patty.

"It was a yucky party with yucky cake
and yucky presents," Dixie grumbled.
"And Bonkety-head kept crying."

"You shouldn't have thrown the cake at
her."

"I don't care," said Dixie. "Nobody loves
me anymore. I wish I lived somewhere
else. I want a new home."

6

The Petersens

THE NEXT DAY WAS THURSDAY. Patty's relatives, the Petersens, were coming.

"Remember everything I told you," said Hilary as Patty got dressed. Hilary had selected Patty's outfit from her own clothing: a fluffy pink sweater, a ruffled flower-print skirt, and white tights.

"Now, let me hear you laugh," said Hilary.

Patty threw back her head and tittered.

"You forgot to cover your mouth," Hilary reminded her. "Otherwise, it was perfect." She combed Patty's hair and sighed. "This hair is hopeless. We'll try the side-ponytail again."

"Okay," Patty agreed. She thought the side-ponytail looked dumb. But Hilary knew best about these things.

Olivia and Collette came to the door. "They just pulled up," Collette said anxiously.

Patty's heart flip-flopped.

"How do they look?" asked Hilary.

"Old," said Collette.

"But okay," Olivia added quickly. "I mean, old, but nice. I mean, maybe. We couldn't really tell."

Patty stood. "How do I look?"

"Like Hilary," Collette and Olivia answered together.

"But that's good," said Olivia. "Since adults like Hilary."

"Oh, man, I'll never understand adults," Collette muttered.

Olivia poked her. "The important thing is to do what works. Don't make Patty more nervous than she is."

"I'm okay," said Patty quietly.

Hilary frowned. "Your voice. Remember your new voice."

"That's right," said Patty in a high, whispery voice.

"Too weird," objected Collette.

"It is not," insisted Hilary. "It's ladylike — something *you* wouldn't know anything about."

The doorbell rang. *Flipflipflopflop* went Patty's heart once again. "It will be fine," said Olivia, squeezing Patty's arm gently.

"Just do everything I said," Hilary coached.

Patty, Olivia, Collette, and Hilary ran to the top of the stairs. They huddled together, trying to see the couple who had arrived with Mrs. Taylor.

Collette was right. They did look very old. The man's coat seemed too big for him. The woman was thin, with short white hair. She wore a round, black hat.

"Hello," Mrs. Baker greeted them. "My husband will be here soon. He has a late class today at the college."

"It's important that we meet him," said

Mrs. Petersen in a crackly voice. "We want to see what type of man he is."

"Of course," said Mrs. Baker, taking their coats.

"Mom sure sounds nervous," Collette noted.

"She's not the only one," Patty whispered.

Hilary gave Patty a small shove. "What are you waiting for? Let's go on down."

Patty bit her thumbnail. Then she took her thumb from her mouth and headed down the stairs. "Chin up, shoulders back," Hilary whispered behind her.

"And don't worry," whispered Collette. "We'll be right outside the door, watching."

Once she got to the living room, Patty went directly to Mrs. Baker's side.

"Patty, these are your cousins, Mr. and Mrs. Petersen," said Mrs. Baker.

"Please call us Aunt Millie and Uncle Hubert," the old woman said. "Doesn't she have Alex's eyes," she murmured to her husband. "And his hair."

Patty knew Alex was her father's name. She opened her mouth. No sound came out. "Patty is shy at first," said Mrs. Taylor.

Uh-oh! thought Patty. She was acting like herself. But she was supposed to be acting like Hilary.

Patty straightened her shoulders and lifted her chin. She *had* to act like Hilary. Her life depended on it. "Oh, no, Mrs. Taylor," said Patty in her whispery voice. "I'm not shy anymore." Patty then smiled brightly in a way she hoped was charming.

"Is your throat sore, dear?" Mrs. Baker asked.

"No, why do you ask?"

"You sound a little hoarse."

Patty had to think quickly. She'd forgotten to warn her mother about her new voice.

Covering her mouth, Patty tittered with laughter. "Oh, Mother, you are such a joker!" She turned to the Petersens. "She is *always* teasing me about my voice."

Mr. and Mrs. Petersen exchanged quick, disapproving glances.

"Teasing might be the wrong word," Patty added quickly. "It's not mean teasing, just funny teasing. It's hysterical, really."

Mrs. Baker looked worried. "I'd like to speak to Patty alone for a minute," she said.

"We'd rather you didn't," said Mr. Petersen. "We'd like to hear what the child has to say for herself."

"Patty," said Mrs. Taylor. "Tell Mr. and Mrs. Petersen what you like best about living here."

How would Hilary answer that question? Patty wondered. Patty had to try very hard to be Hilary. The problem was, Hilary was always complaining.

Patty put her hand on one hip — Hilary-style. With the other, she flipped her ponytail. "It is *such* a madhouse here. It's absolutely chaos, but I do like my ballet lessons."

"Ballet lessons?" asked Mrs. Baker, surprised.

"Yes, you know, Mother, my ballet lessons," Patty insisted pointedly.

"Were you unaware that Patty was taking ballet lessons?" Mrs. Petersen questioned Mrs. Baker.

"Well, frankly, I — " Mrs. Baker stammered, casting a nervous eye on Patty.

"Oh, please," Patty cut in. "Of course, she forgets things like that. I mean, she has thirteen kids, after all. Who wouldn't forget?"

"Hmmmm," muttered Mrs. Petersen. "Perhaps thirteen children is more than you and your husband can handle."

"Not at all," said Mrs. Baker firmly. "We have no trouble — "

Just then, Chris stuck her head into the living room. "I'm really sorry, Mom, but have you seen Dixie? I can't find her anywhere."

"Weren't you watching her?" asked Mrs. Baker.

"I answered the phone. I turned my back for just one second to write down a number, and she was gone," Chris explained.

"Check down in the basement," said Mrs. Baker.

Chris left, and Mrs. Baker turned her attention back to the Petersens. "As I was saying, some people might think thirteen is a problem, but — "

From upstairs, Addie began to wail. Grannie Baker scurried past the doorway. "Don't worry. I've got her," she said, stopping briefly. "You go on talking with Patty. What a lovely child! It would break our hearts to see her leave. Break them right in two."

Outside in the yard, Jojo began to howl.

"Mom," Mrs. Baker reminded Grannie. "Addie."

"Oh, yes, yes," said Grannie, climbing up the stairs. "I almost forgot. Addie."

"How are you doing in school?" Mrs. Petersen asked Patty.

"Great," said Patty. "I'm extremely popular." She went on to tell Mrs. Petersen about all the kids in her class, adding little bits of gossip she hoped would be interesting.

As she spoke, she was aware that all her brothers and sisters were passing back and forth in the hallway. "I've already looked in the basement," she heard Chris say.

"She wouldn't go into the woods by herself, would she?" Mark asked. "She knows she's not allowed."

"Excuse me a moment," said Mrs. Baker, leaving the room.

"Patty, tell the Petersens about some of your favorite hobbies," said Mrs. Taylor.

Again, Patty tried to think like Hilary. She talked about loving clothing and fashion magazines as Hilary did — but she found it hard to think about what she was saying. Instead, she was thinking about Dixie. What could have happened to her?

Mr. Baker came into the living room. "Hello, everyone," he said. "Sorry to be late. I'm Tom Baker."

"Tom, I need to talk to you," said Mrs. Baker from the hallway. Patty listened, but couldn't make out their words.

"I'll take the van," Mr. Baker said to Mrs. Baker as he headed back toward the door. "Maybe she walked up the road." He stopped himself and returned to the living room. "Slight family emergency," he explained to the Petersens. "My wife and I will be right back. With thirteen kids, it's always something."

"Yes, so it seems," Mrs. Petersen said, casting another skeptical glance at her husband.

Mr. Baker didn't hear her. He was out the door.

"You were telling us about your love of fashion," Mrs. Taylor reminded Patty.

"What?" asked Patty. Suddenly, her whole act seemed very wrong. She couldn't stand there talking about some made-up hobbies for another minute. Not when Dixie was missing.

Then it came to her. She knew where Dixie might have gone.

"I'm sorry. I can't talk anymore," she said to the Petersens as she ran from the room. She used her own voice, not her whispery one. "I have to find my sister."

7

Trapped!

PATTY RAN INTO THE BACKYARD. "Mom!" she called. "Mom!"

"Just a minute," Mrs. Baker's voice came from the woods. She stepped out from the trees. "Why aren't you inside with the Petersens?" she asked Patty.

"She wants to look for her sister," said Mrs. Taylor, stepping out the back door. The Petersens were right behind her. "Can we help?"

"I think I know where she is," said Patty excitedly. "Dixie told me she thought it

60

would be fun to live in the old car we found."

"Come on," said Mrs. Baker. Patty and her mother ran into the woods. All around, the Baker kids searched for Dixie, calling her name. "We'll let them keep looking," Mrs. Baker said to Patty. "Just in case she's not at the car."

Patty led the way. She hoped she could remember exactly where the car was. At some points, she thought she might be going in the wrong direction. But after almost five minutes, she came to the slope. "It's down here," she told Mrs. Baker.

They looked down the slope. A shaft of sunlight fell right on the car. "Dixie!" Mrs. Baker called. "Dixie!"

"Dixie!" Patty echoed. There was no reply.

Patty and her mother scrambled down the slope toward the car. They stopped and listened. Birds chirped. Now and then a branch snapped as some small creature ran by.

Then, suddenly, they heard it.

"Help! Help!"

Patty and Mrs. Baker looked at one another. The voice was muffled. "Where is she?" asked Patty.

"Mommy! Mommy!"

"The trunk!" cried Mrs. Baker. "She's in the trunk!" They ran to the back of the car. "We'll get you out, honey," said Mrs. Baker, tugging at the trunk door. It wouldn't budge. Mrs. Baker's face turned red as she strained to open it. Still, it wouldn't move.

Just then, Mrs. Taylor and the Petersens appeared at the top of the slope. "She's stuck in the trunk," Mrs. Baker called to them. "I can't open it."

"I'll call the police," said Mrs. Taylor, running back toward the house.

The Petersens held hands and slowly made their way down the slope.

Inside the trunk, Dixie began to cry. "Mommy, Mommy, I'm scared. Get me out."

"We'll get you out. Be brave, sweetie," said Mrs. Baker.

"Oh, dear," said Mrs. Petersen when she reached the car. "I hope she has enough air."

Air? Patty looked at her mother. Could Dixie smother in there?

"The police will be here soon," said Mrs. Baker.

Mr. Petersen took a penknife from his pocket. "I bet I can spring the lock with this," he said. There were lots of parts to his knife. One was a skinny little blade. He knelt and fiddled with the lock. Patty looked at him hopefully. "Darn," he said after a moment. "This isn't going to work."

"Where are those police?" Mrs. Baker fretted.

Patty walked to the side of the car. She looked at the almost half-open window. "I have an idea," she said. "If we can get into the car, maybe we can pull Dixie out through the back dashboard. Look. It's all crumbly and has a bunch of holes in it already."

"That means the child can breathe," said Mrs. Petersen.

"Yes," said Mrs. Baker, smiling for a moment. "That's true."

Mrs. Baker pulled on the door, but it wouldn't open. Sticking her head in through the open window, she pulled up the lock. The door still wouldn't open. "It must be rusted shut," she said.

Mr. Petersen tried to open the doors. He banged the locks with a heavy rock. All three adults tried to pull on one of the doors at once. It was no use.

"Maybe I can squeeze through the window," Patty suggested.

Mrs. Baker looked at the window doubtfully. "I don't think you can get through," she said. Mrs. Baker used all her strength to push the window down. It went down about an inch and then wouldn't go any farther.

Mr. Petersen held up his rock. "I can break the window," he suggested.

"But someone will still have to crawl through, and that would be dangerous if there's broken glass all around," said Mrs. Petersen.

"I think I can get through now," said Patty.

Mrs. Baker lifted her. First she stuck her feet and legs in. That was no problem. But her stomach got wedged for a moment. She sucked in her breath and moved forward another inch. "Are you all right?" asked Mrs. Baker, who was holding her by her shoulders.

"Mommy! Get me out!" Dixie wailed.

"I'm okay," said Patty. Finally, her shoulders and head squeezed through the window. "Hey, Dixie," Patty called through the opening in the back dashboard. "I'll have you out in a minute."

Patty dug her fingers into a hole in the rotted wood. It was a flakey board, but it was thicker than it looked. "Use this," said Mr. Petersen, handing his penknife to Patty through the window.

Opening the blade, Patty hacked at the board. Slowly the hole got bigger and bigger. But it was a lot of work. And it took all her strength. "Don't cry, Dixie," she said soothingly as she worked. "You're okay now. Everything is okay."

Dixie stopped crying. "I wanted to close the door to my house," she explained. "But I couldn't open it again."

"You'll be out̄ soon," said Patty. Her arm began to ache. Then her shoulder hurt. Still, she kept on going. She had to get Dixie out.

Mrs. Baker and the Petersens looked in the windows. "How are you doing?" asked Mrs. Baker.

"This is going to take forever," replied Patty, but, suddenly she hit a weak spot in the board. It cracked as soon as she touched it with the knife. "Push, Dix, push," she called as she yanked up the board. Dixie pounded on the board from underneath.

Creee-aa-aaakkkk! The board split and split again. Soon they'd made an opening wide enough for Dixie to squeeze through.

"You did it!" cried Dixie, poking her head up through the hole. "I knew you could."

"Are you okay?" Patty asked, wrapping

her arms around Dixie and pulling. Strands of Dixie's blonde hair stuck to her sweaty forehead. Her eyes were red and puffy from crying. Other than that, she seemed fine.

"Dixie!" cried Mrs. Baker. "Thank goodness."

Patty knelt on the seat and helped guide Dixie through the window to Mrs. Baker.

When Dixie was through, Patty leaned forward, preparing to go next. She noticed her knee was dirty. Looking down, she saw that she'd been kneeling on the weed that grew in the patch of dirt on the ripped seat. It lay, bent over. Tenderly, Patty plumped the dirt back up around it. She propped it up against the back seat. It had come this far; she didn't want anything to happen to it now.

Mrs. Baker helped Patty out of the car and hugged her. "Good work," she said. Mrs. Baker turned to the Petersens. "Thanks for your help."

"You're welcome," said Mrs. Petersen. Her voice was kind, but she wasn't smiling.

As they headed up the slope, they were met by all the Baker kids. Mark was in the front. "She's all right," he called back to the other kids. "The police just got here," he told his mother. "Dad is bringing them to the car."

Soon, Mr. Baker, the police, Mrs. Taylor, and all the kids crowded around Dixie. "Why did you go off by yourself?" Mrs. Baker asked Dixie.

Dixie looked at the ground. "Nobody loves me anymore," she said quietly.

"Oh, Dixie," sighed Mr. Baker. "We love you. Forever and always."

Something in Mr. Baker's tone made Patty look over at the Petersens. They were standing off to the side, talking seriously. They were frowning and shaking their heads.

Icy fingers of fear ran up Patty's back. She didn't like the looks on their faces. Not one bit.

8

Saying Good-bye

PATTY SAT ON THE BAKERS' big bed. Mr. Baker wore a serious expression. Mrs. Baker's eyes were red, as if she'd been crying. She wasn't crying now, though. She just looked very, very sad.

It was Saturday morning. Mrs. Baker had asked her to come into the room to have a talk.

Patty could barely breathe. She knew what was coming.

Mr. Baker sat on the bed next to her. He took her small hand in his large one.

69

Patty remembered how he'd shaken hands with her the evening she'd first arrived. She'd thought he had the biggest hands she'd ever seen. And the kindest eyes.

"Mrs. Taylor called us this morning," Mr. Baker began. "It seems that the Petersens want you to come live with them."

Tears sprang to Patty's eyes. She'd been expecting it — but, somehow she'd never really believed it would happen. "Why?" she cried. "Why do they want me? They don't even know me!"

"They think things in this house are a little too crazy," said Mrs. Baker. "They think thirteen is too many kids." Mrs. Baker put her hand over her mouth and gazed at the ceiling. Patty knew she was trying hard not to cry.

"I won't go!" Patty said. "I won't. I'll run away and I'll come back here."

Mr. and Mrs. Baker looked at one another. There was great sorrow in their eyes. "Mrs. Taylor says that there's not much we can do. Your adoption isn't final, and they *are* your blood relatives," Mr.

70

Baker said. "They seem like nice people. They're only doing this because they think you'll have a better life with them."

"I'll have a terrible life!" Patty sobbed. "It's not fair!"

"She's right," said Mrs. Baker, a fat tear rolling down her cheek. "It's not fair!"

"Ann, remember, we said we'd stay calm," said Mr. Baker.

"I'm calm! I'm calm!" Mrs. Baker said in a voice that wasn't calm at all. She wiped her eyes and looked at the ceiling again. "Okay, now I really am calm," she said after a couple of deep breaths. "But I want to talk to Mr. and Mrs. Petersen. I have to tell them that they can't do this. I'll get Patty's teachers to call. They'll say how well Patty does in school, and how everyone likes her."

"It's worth trying," said Mr. Baker. "We can't promise anything, Patty. But we'll try."

"Listen, sweetheart. I have to ask you something," said Mrs. Baker. "Why did you act so . . . so . . . strange when the

71

Petersens were here? You know, saying you took ballet lessons and talking in that odd voice. Do you know why you did that?"

Patty suddenly felt very foolish. "I wasn't acting strange. I was acting like Hilary."

"Like Hilary?" Mr. Baker cried softly. "Why?"

"Adults like Hilary," Patty explained. "I wanted the Petersens to like me so they'd see I was a perfect kid and then they'd let me stay."

Mr. Baker sighed wearily.

Mrs. Baker shook her head sadly. "That was Hilary's bright idea, wasn't it?" she guessed.

"Sort of," Patty admitted. "But I thought it was a good idea, too. At least, at the time I did."

Mrs. Baker took a piece of paper off her dresser. The Petersens were staying at the nearby Wild Falls Motel. Mrs. Petersen had left their phone number. "Sweetheart, let me talk to the Petersens alone," said Mrs. Baker as she picked up the phone receiver. "Maybe if I can explain some of this, they will change their minds."

Patty got off the bed. Hilary was waiting for her outside in the hall. "Bad news?" she asked.

Nodding, Patty headed up to their bedroom on the third floor. Hilary followed. When they reached their room, the rest of the kids were sitting in the hallway outside.

"What happened?" asked Kenny.

Patty looked at each of them. They'd all seemed so strange when she'd first arrived. Now they were so familiar. Almost like a part of her. They were her brothers and sisters. She couldn't leave them. "I . . . um . . ." she began. "The Petersens want me to . . . I . . ." She couldn't say the words. Instead, she ran past them into her bedroom.

"They want her," Hilary confirmed.

The kids were in an uproar. They rushed into Patty and Hilary's room.

"They can't!" cried Olivia.

"They're fiends!" said Hilary.

"We'll hide you," suggested Howie.

"Great idea!" said Kenny. "You can live in my old tree house for a while. I'll fix it up for you."

"We'll bring you food every day," said Terry.

"I'll move in with you, so you don't get lonely," Collette volunteered.

"I'll move in with her," Hilary objected. "I'm her main sister, after all."

"You are not," protested Olivia.

"Am so," said Hilary. "Patty and I share a room."

"We're all her brothers and sisters," Chris said firmly. "And you can't hide her in the tree house. The police will find her. Besides, it might get Mom and Dad in trouble."

Everyone fell silent. Until this moment, Patty had never realized how much they all loved her. Really, really loved her. And — since she'd arrived — she'd been so busy that she hadn't stopped to think about how much she loved them. Each of them.

Patty noticed Jack quietly crying in the corner. Dixie had put her arm around him, but she, too, was sniffling.

"Maybe Mom will talk the Petersens out of it," said Mark hopefully. "She can be pretty convincing."

"Let's listen in and hear what she's saying," Chris suggested. The kids followed Chris to her room. She was the only one with an extension phone. Carefully, she lifted the phone off the hook. All the kids crowded around, trying to listen.

Chris cupped her hand over the receiver. "Dad's talking to Ms. Sherman. She wants her to call Mrs. Petersen and let her know how well Patty is doing in school. Ms. Sherman says she will."

"The Petersens will listen to Ms. Sherman," said Olivia. "She's a teacher."

The other kids nodded as Chris listened again. "They're calling someone else," Chris told the kids. "It's the school principal." Chris listened a while longer. "Oh, uh, okay, Mom," she said. "Mom told me to get off the line," she explained.

For the next few hours, the kids continued to listen. They picked up the phone and discovered that Mrs. Baker was again talking to Mrs. Petersen. Chris laid the phone on the bed so they could all hear.

"Mrs. Taylor is drawing up the papers we need this weekend," Mrs. Petersen told Mrs. Baker. "We'll be taking Patty to Nebraska on Monday. Tuesday the latest. She needs to be with her family."

"But she's part of our family now," Mrs. Baker pleaded.

"I understand," said Mrs. Petersen. "But it seems to me that you have your hands quite full. There seems to be a certain amount of chaos in your home."

"Maybe, but the kids are all well taken care of, I assure you that — "

"Mrs. Baker, your child locked herself in the trunk of a car."

"We found her. We knew she was missing right away, and she wasn't hurt."

"What if you hadn't found her?" said Mrs. Petersen.

"But we did," Mrs. Baker argued. "Kids are always doing crazy things like that. It's part of being a kid."

"I'm sorry, I just think you have too many children. I'm concerned that Patty is not getting the attention she needs."

"That's not true," said Mrs. Baker.

"Forgive me, but you were not even aware that Patty takes ballet lessons."

"She doesn't take ballet lessons," Mrs. Baker said. "I can explain about that. Patty was trying to act like one of her sisters."

"Yes, she showed two very different personalities," said Mrs. Petersen. "I'd say that was the sign of a disturbed child."

"I told you she shouldn't try to be like Hilary," said Collette. "They thought she was disturbed."

"Shhh," said Chris.

"Patty is not disturbed," Mrs. Baker argued. "She just thought that her sister Hilary had a personality you would like better. She wanted you to think she was a perfect child so that she could stay here."

"Then she obviously feels there is something wrong with her own personality," said Mrs. Petersen. "That is not a healthy sign, either."

"Oh, come on," said Mrs. Baker, beginning to lose her temper. "She's a child. She wanted you to like her so she could stay here, where she's happy. She was desperate. Can't you see that?"

There was silence for a moment. When Mrs. Petersen finally spoke, her voice was cold. "Please have Patty packed and ready."

With a click, Mrs. Petersen hung up.

There was no hope. Olivia put her arm around Patty. "This is awful," Olivia said.

"How can they be so mean?" asked Terry.

"I don't know," said Mark.

Suddenly a horrible sickness welled up inside Patty. She cupped her hand over her mouth and ran out of Chris's room and down the hall to the bathroom.

9

Forever and Ever

PATTY CRIED HERSELF TO SLEEP on Saturday night. She clutched her rag doll, Zanzibar Marie. The doll had been her best friend through two foster homes and a stay at a children's shelter. She still loved the doll, but lately she'd stopped sleeping with her. Tonight she took Zanzibar Marie off the shelf and held her tight.

Sometimes Patty dozed for a short while. Then she'd awaken. For a few groggy seconds, she'd forget what had happened. Everything seemed fine. Then she'd remember — and start crying all over again.

One time, just as she woke, she heard Hilary crying. Her blanket was over her head, but Patty could still hear her sobbing. "Hilary," she called softly.

Hilary's head popped up from the blanket.

"Will you write to me?" Patty asked.

Hilary ran across the room. She wrapped Patty in a hug. "Of course, I'll write to you. You'd be a mess without my advice," she cried.

The two of them sat in the dark crying with their arms around one another. Soon their door cracked open. It was Collette and Olivia. "We couldn't sleep," said Collette.

"We just wanted to come look at you," said Olivia, bursting into tears. The two girls ran to Patty's bed and climbed on.

"Let's all sleep together tonight," said Collette. She and Hilary pushed the two beds together, and the four of them climbed in.

Patty felt herself slipping into the crack between the beds. She didn't mind. With her sisters so close, it seemed as if nothing could hurt her.

The morning was different, though. That's when the dreamy feeling began. She felt as if she were walking in her sleep and nothing was real. "She's in shock," she heard Grannie say to Mr. Baker.

Mrs. Baker brought Patty a suitcase. She put it on Patty's bed, then she knelt and hugged Patty tight. "We will always love you," she said. "We'll write to you. You'll be in our hearts forever and ever. No matter what, don't forget that."

Patty nodded. It all seemed so unreal.

Mrs. Baker leaned back, holding Patty's arms. "Your cousins are good people. Try to be happy with them. Don't waste time thinking about the things you don't like. Find things to like. Be happy, Patty."

"I . . . I'll try," Patty said in a faint voice.

Mrs. Baker opened the suitcase, stared at it for a moment, and then shut it. "We'll pack later," she said. "There will be enough time later."

That afternoon, the Bakers had an extra-special dinner. Roast turkey, candied sweet potatoes, cranberry sauce, and creamed spinach — the one vegetable Patty liked. "It looks like Thanksgiving," Dixie said.

"But it feels like doomsday," grumbled Mark as he took his seat.

"Please," said Mr. Baker. "Let's try to have a nice dinner."

Everyone ate quietly. No one felt much like talking. Especially Patty. The delicious meal lay like clumps of sawdust in her mouth.

Then the phone rang.

Everyone looked at one another.

"Now what?" sighed Grannie Baker.

Mr. Baker got up and answered it. "Yes, certainly. By all means," he spoke into the phone. "That was Mrs. Petersen."

"What did that old hag want?" asked Kenny angrily.

"Kenny!" Mrs. Baker scolded. "She's Patty's cousin and I'm sure she believes she's doing the right thing."

"She wants to talk to us," Mr. Baker said as he took his seat.

"Is she taking Patty?" Dixie cried, panicked. "Is she coming to take her?"

"No," said Mr. Baker. "She needs the paperwork. She can't get that until Monday."

"What if Mrs. Taylor worked the weekend and mailed it to her?" asked Chris.

"Let's eat," said Mr. Baker. The family tried, but they couldn't pretend everything was normal. Even Jojo sensed something was wrong. When Addie began crying in her stroller, he lifted his head, but he didn't howl along.

In a half hour, the doorbell rang. "I'll get it," said Mr. Baker.

"Watch the baby, please, Mom," said Mrs. Baker to Grannie as she followed her husband from the kitchen.

One at a time, the kids got up from the

table and gathered around the kitchen door. Even Grannie scooped up Addie and joined them.

Patty stayed in her seat. She felt as though she couldn't move. "Come on," said Hilary, pulling her arm. "Let's hear what they're saying."

The Bakers invited Mrs. Petersen into the living room. Silently, the rest of the family sneaked down the hall to listen.

"Forgive me for coming over without much notice," Mrs. Petersen began primly. "I wanted to see your house and talk to you one more time. I needed to double-check my first impressions."

"Your first impressions were wrong," said Mr. Baker.

"Maybe. Maybe not," Mrs. Petersen replied tartly. "I think there are too many children here. I've made up my mind about that. But two things have been disturbing me all morning. For one, I can't stop seeing the image of Patty as she worked to free her little sister. She was quite impressive."

"Patty really loves Dixie," said Mrs. Baker.

"Yes. That much was clear," Mrs. Petersen admitted stiffly.

"That was the real Patty," Mrs. Baker went on.

"Perhaps. Now, tell me again. Who was this person Patty was trying to be like? That's the second thing I need to understand more clearly."

Suddenly, Hilary ran out from her hiding place in the hallway. "It was all my dumb idea," she cried, running into the living room. "I told her to be like me. But she didn't get it right."

Mrs. Petersen's eyes went wide with surprise. She looked at Mrs. Baker. "Who is *this*?"

"This is Hilary, our daughter," Mrs. Baker told her.

"You see, I can act like me and everyone likes it, but on Patty it looked weird. But the real Patty is great." Hilary went on. "If you got to know her, you'd see that she's not disturbed at all. You'd like her. I love her, and I want her to stay — even if it means I don't have my own room. So don't blame Patty because of my stupid idea."

"That's very sweet, dear," said Mrs. Petersen. "But I must consider Patty's welfare, and I don't — "

Pressed against the hallway wall, Patty listened. Now it was time to speak. She stepped into the entrance of the living room. "I want to stay," she said in a small, shaky voice.

"Speak up, dear, I can't hear you," said Mrs. Petersen.

Patty froze.

"She said she wants to stay," Hilary said softly.

Patty nodded as tears rolled down her cheeks. "Please don't make me go. Please don't make me." Her voice choked in her throat and she stood there, trembling with emotion.

Mrs. Petersen got up and crossed the room until she was standing in front of Patty. She unclipped her purse, took a starched white handkerchief from it, and handed it to Patty.

"Can you tell me why you want to stay?" she asked.

Patty wiped her eyes. "Because they love me, and I love them. This is *my* family. I belong here."

Mrs. Petersen patted Patty on the shoulder. Then she turned to Mr. and Mrs. Baker. "I'm not a person who lets emotions get in the way of common sense," she said. "But clearly you want the child to stay. And Patty has now made it quite clear that she wishes to stay. Despite what you may think, I'm not a heartless person. I only wanted to do the right thing. I'm glad I came back for a second look. Now I see more clearly what the right thing is."

"Are you saying she can stay?" asked Mrs. Baker.

"That's what I'm saying," said Mrs. Petersen.

"Yes! Yes!" cried Collette, leaping out from the hallway.

"Yip-yip-yahoooooooooooooo!" yelled Kenny.

The kids jumped and cheered as they tumbled into the living room. Terry turned a cartwheel. Howie and Kevin grabbed one another and spun in a circle. Hilary, Olivia, and Collette crushed Patty in a hug. "You're staying!" cried Hilary, dragging Patty into the living room.

But still Patty couldn't feel anything. Not happy. Not sad. Nothing.

"May I have a moment alone with Patty?" Mrs. Petersen asked.

"Yes, oh, yes," said Mrs. Baker, smiling brightly. "Come on, children. Let's go."

In a moment, all the Baker kids had gone. Patty was alone with Mrs. Petersen. Her cousin brushed Patty's hair lightly. "Don't you ever forget that you have family in Nebraska. If you ever need us, you call or write. We love you, too."

"I'll remember," said Patty.

"And maybe you can come out and visit during the summer. We have a small farm, you know."

"That would be nice," Patty said quietly.

"We only wanted what was best for you," said Mrs. Petersen. "We didn't mean to upset you. I'm glad you are happy here."

"Yes, I am happy," Patty said. "Very happy." Suddenly, it was as if a dam burst inside her. The dreaminess was gone. The danger had passed. She was safe. It was safe to feel happy again.

A wild gush of joy rose up in her. "Thank you! Thank you for letting me stay," she told her cousin.

"You're welcome," said Mrs. Petersen. She gently kissed Patty on the cheek. "Good-bye," she said, and quietly let herself out the front door. In the next moment, the family rushed into the living room.

"Now you can be adopted, Patty!" cried Terry.

"You'll be a Baker forever and ever!" added Howie.

"Forever and ever," Patty echoed, smiling. "And ever and ever and ever."

12 times the fun with...

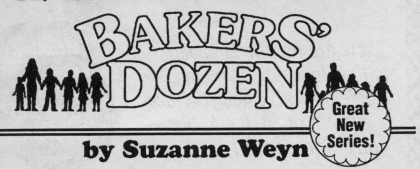

BAKERS' DOZEN

Great New Series!

by Suzanne Weyn

❏ NL43559-0 **#1 Make Room for Patty**   **$2.75**

Eight-year-old Patty Conners has wanted a home and a loving family ever since her mother died three years ago. She gets her wish when the Bakers adopt her. But will one of her new sisters spoil it all?

❏ NL43560-4 **#2 Hilary and the Rich Girl**   **$2.75**

Hilary's new classmate Alice has everything — a big house, beautiful dresses, and great toys. Now Hilary wants to be her friend — at any cost!

❏ NL43562-0 **#3 Collette's Magic Star**   **$2.75**

Kenny has a terrible accident and is going blind. He needs an operation but there's no promise it will cure him. Can Collette and her magic star help Kenny see again?

Watch for new titles every three months!

Available wherever you buy books, or use this order form.

Scholastic Inc., P.O. Box 7502, 2931 East McCarty Street, Jefferson City, MO 65102

Please send me the books I have checked above. I am enclosing $_____ (please add $2.00 to cover shipping and handling). Send check or money order — no cash or C.O.D.s please.

Name _____

Address _____

City_____ State/Zip _____

Please allow four to six weeks for delivery. Available in the U.S. only. Sorry, mail orders are not available to residents of Canada. Prices subject to change.

BD1190